Short Stories

Short Stories

Monekka L. Munroe

Short Stories

Great Minds Publishing
www.greatmindspublishing.com
greatmindspublishing@gmail.com

Printed in the USA
First Printing in 2017

Library of Congress Control Number: 2017919237
ISBN-10: 0989005046
ISBN-13: 978-0-9890050-4-3

Edited by Mrs. Aariel Munroe-Simpkins

There will be times when peace is more powerful than understanding.

Table of Contents

It Could Have Been Me

That was an incredible party! Now, I have to clean this mess, but not tonight, in the morning. Tonight, I am going to bed, Rocka thought as she walked toward her dogs. As she was removing the muzzles from her two blue nose pitbulls, Nada and Chance, she heard a knock on her door. As she walked to the door, she asked who was there and to her surprise it was a guest from the party, a guy who called himself Blade. Shocked that was he was there at such a late hour, Rocka talked to him through the door and asked, "What's up?"

Blade laughed and explained, "I think I left my cell phone in your apartment."

"Just a second," said Rocka as she unlocked and opened the door. When Blade entered the apartment, he noticed Nada and Chance standing guard in the living room area. Blade immediately tells her that he is deathly afraid of dogs and pleads with her to put them in another room so that he can look for his phone. He continues to explain that he feels so ashamed to reveal his fear of dogs to her because she is so beautiful and he wanted to ask her for her phone number the entire time he was at the party.

Rocka, on the other hand, not interested at all, told him that she was not willing to put her dogs in another room because neither she nor the dogs really know him. She explained that although he was a guest at her party earlier in the evening, she doesn't know him well enough to be alone in the apartment with him. She did offer however, to look for his phone while he stood outside of her apartment door. Blade, looked confused by her statements and immediately stated, "Really?"

Rocka responded, "Yes, really."

As he walked toward the door, Rocka asked him for his phone number offering to call it from her phone to find it quicker. He stated that he was pretty sure his ringer was turned off. As she led him out of the door, she assured him that she would find the phone if indeed it was in her apartment. She asked him to give her about ten minutes. She closed and locked her door. Rocka then called her brother and his roommate who attended the party earlier and asked them to come back to her apartment to help find Blade's missing phone.

Mike and Julian arrived about two minutes after the call. Rocka could hear the men talking to Blade outside of her apartment door, and to her surprise, she heard Blade tell them he found his phone. He didn't realize it was in his car the entire time. Rocka then opened the door and Blade tried to explain to her about the phone and then apologized for coming back to the apartment at 1:30 a.m. They all laughed and she told him she was glad he found the phone. She also thanked Mike and Julian for coming over to assist, and then said she was tired and needed to get some rest. She watched as all three men walked toward the parking lot. She then closed and locked her door. Next, she checked the window locks, placed food and water in two bowls for Nada and Chance. As she sat on her bed and turned on the television, she felt proud of herself for taking those precautions while Blade was in her apartment. She thought to herself that he was handsome, but she also thought it was strange that he waited until everyone had left before returning to look for his phone. She also wondered if he was truly as afraid of dogs as he appeared to be. Either way, she was glad her brother taught her to trust her instincts.

A picture she saw on the news interrupted her thoughts. The news anchor was reporting about two rapes that occurred last week. The picture was a drawing of the suspect, and although Rocka was not 100% sure, her gut instinct was telling her that she was looking at a picture of Blade, the guy who just left her apartment! She was stunned! She immediately called Mike and Julian and told them to turn their TV to the local news channel. They saw the picture and both yelled simultaneously, "Hell no!"

Rocka then said, "That's him, right?" Both men agreed the picture on the screen was indeed Blade. After the call ended, Rocka sat in shock. She wondered if he was planning to make her his next victim; if perhaps, he was planning to kill her; maybe he was planning to come back or was it possible that he was still outside? Her mind was racing, and she could not calm down. She reached in the drawer beside her bed to retrieve her Glock 357 and made sure it was loaded. Once again, she checked the door and window locks, and performed a final walk-through of her apartment with Nada and Chance by her side the entire time.

Knowing that her dogs and her Glock were in the bedroom with her, Rocka was able to relax and finally get some much-needed rest. The next morning, there was an insistent knock on her door. As Chance barked loudly, Rocka jumped out of bed, grabbed her robe and her Glock, and walked toward the door. She yelled, "Who is it?"

Relieved, she heard Mike's voice, "It's me, Sis. Open up." She calmed Chance, placed her Glock in the case, and opened the door for Mike. As he walked in, he said, "I know you heard that shit about Blade, right?"

Rocka said, "Yeah, I called you about it last night, remember?"

"No," Mike said. "Some other shit went down after that. Apparently, after he left your place, he went to some other girl house. She let him in and he tried to rape her, but she wasn't having that shit. She shot and killed him!"

The Set-Up

This job is a true blessing. I love what I do, the people I work with are very nice, and I really enjoy helping others. This is such a great opportunity, I'm so blessed.

Today, I walked into the break room and saw Michelle. She was complaining about having a migraine headache. I asked if there was anything I could do to help and she said no. I told her that I suffer from migraines from time to time and I found quick relief with some new pain pills prescribed by my neurologist. Michelle said she believes her pain is the result of stress. She explained that she had applied for a promotion at the office and was really nervous about it. She said everyone told her she probably wouldn't get the position because she did not have a graduate degree, but she disagreed, explaining that her extensive experience in the field should more than qualify her for the promotion.

I felt bad for her because while I was trying to comfort her and encourage her to follow her dreams, I knew that I too had applied for the same position. I applied at the request of a senior manager who was aware that I completed my graduate degree last year. The candidate is supposed to be notified next week.

Wednesday morning was rough. It was hot and humid, the air conditioner in my car was acting crazy, and everyone wanted to drive as if they were in a Christmas parade. I was hot, sweaty, and frustrated, and it was only 9:00 a.m. Crazy day already. When I finally arrived at the office, I noticed a couple of ladies standing near Michelle, it seemed as if she was crying or at the very least upset about something. I walked over and asked if everything was ok, and Michelle looked me and almost yelled, "Bitch please!"

I stood back, looked at the ladies and said, "What?" Michelle walked away. Confused, I walked to my desk where I saw a bouquet of roses, balloons, and a card. I was shocked because I had no idea what the gifts were for or who left them. I opened the card and it read 'congratulations on the new promotion, well deserved.' I had no idea. However, it became crystal clear why Michelle reacted the way she did earlier. She assumed I knew the position was mine and pretended to care about her feelings. I immediately went to her desk to talk with her, but she told me to go away. Hurt, I left her sitting there in tears.

My new supervisor came to my desk to welcome me to the new team and to show me my new office space. My excitement was diminished by Michelle's sadness, I felt bad for her and did not want there to be any friction between the two of us. When I arrived at home, I shared the news with my daughter who was so excited for me. She laughed and said, "Now, you can get a real cell phone and stop carrying that flip phone." For some reason, if I hit the phone against something or dropped it, the recording device is turned on. Weird.

The following week, to my surprise Michelle came to my office to apologize. She explained that it wasn't my fault and that I deserved the promotion. As she was leaving, she began to rub her forehead. "Another migraine," I asked.

She responded, "Yeah, it seems no matter what kind of medication I take, I cannot get rid of this pain. Do you think I can try one of those pain pills prescribed by your doctor?"

I said, "Sure, I have a few of them in my bag, you can have four." She thanked me and walked away. By lunch, she sent me an email thanking me for the pills and explained that she felt much better. I was relieved and I was slowly regaining my excitement. Now, I needed to get rid of some of the things from my old office and prepare to buy new items. I listed some of the furniture as free but other items I was willing to sell. Michelle agreed to buy a couple of furniture pieces along with some wall art. I agreed to sell her everything she wanted for 75.00. That was a relief because I did not want to take that stuff to my new space. Next week I should be all moved in and ready to receive my new work assignments. God is good.

Monday morning, 8:00 sharp, I turned on my computer, opened my email and was about to respond when the phone rang. It was my supervisor asking me to come to her office. When I arrived, there were two police officers standing there. I was asked to have a seat. One of the officers asked if I was Lace Boudreaux, and I said yes. Another officer asked if I could provide valid identification and I did. After looking at my picture I.D. one of the officers informed me that I was being placed under arrest for trafficking, distribution, and sale of a controlled substance. I immediately told them they were making a mistake, I continued explaining that I have never sold drugs to anyone in my life! I asked if I could call an attorney and one of the officers told me I would have a chance to do that at the police station. I was then handcuffed and walked through the hallway in front of my co-workers, embarrassed and confused.

After arriving at the police station, I was fingerprinted, asked if I had anything in my hair and pockets, and then escorted to the desk where my mugshot was taken. I was placed in a cell along with five other women. As I sat there, I couldn't believe this was happening to me. This has to be some kind of mistake. When and who did I sell drugs to? What kind of control substance were they talking about? When the hell am I getting out of here?

One of the women in the cell told me to stop looking dumbfounded and use the phone on the wall to call someone. I called my mother and explained what happened. I told her that I had no idea if I had a bond amount, but I needed her to get me out immediately. After about six hours, one of the correctional officers opened the cell and called my name. As I was leaving the cell, the woman who told me about the phone whispered to me, "Don't forget about us."

I was escorted down a long hall and at the end of it stood my mother, daughter, and best friend. I hugged them and burst into tears, I tried to talk but they had no idea what I was saying. We walked to the car and I calmed down enough to speak fluently. I told them someone made a terrible mistake or someone had lied on me, but either way, I was going to get to the bottom of it.

The next morning, I went to meet the bail bondsman. He explained that I was released after my mom paid 10% of the 10,000.00 bond amount. I had to sign documents promising to appear at all scheduled court dates and agree to not leave town under any circumstance. My next appointment was with an attorney. I was so nervous, I had never interacted with lawyers in the past, and I didn't know what to expect. I definitely didn't want anyone judging or stereotyping me. The last thing I needed to hear was statistics about young, black, single mothers with a criminal record.

My mom contacted this attorney, and she assured me I would like this person. As I entered her office, the attorney looked very familiar, but I was sure I didn't know her. She stood behind her desk and extended her hand as she revealed a warm smile. She asked if I remembered her and I said no. She explained that she and I worked together briefly at a clothing store when we were both undergrad students in college. During that time, she was attending Florida State University and I was a student at Florida A & M University. I thought for a moment, and smiled back. Yes, I remembered her, she always wanted to be a lawyer and looks like she fulfilled her dream. That's awesome. However, right now, I needed her assistance with staying out of prison so that I can continue to fulfill my dreams.

Attorney Tamela Harris handed me a file. In the file was the complaint, police report, and evidence against me. The report stated that I had sold a co-worker nine pain pills for 75.00. The evidence document was the check that was written to me by Michelle! At the bottom of the check she wrote, 'thanks for the pain pills, you saved my life,' and then the bitch had the nerve to draw a smiley face at the end of the sentence! How did I miss that when she handed me the check? Did she set me up because she didn't get the promotion?

"Tamela, Michelle is lying. She did write the check to me, but the money was for some furniture I was selling from my old office. Two other people also bought items from me on the same day. I'm telling you, that chick is lying. She's upset because I was selected for a job promotion that she wanted. I just can't prove it," I explaind.

Tamela then said, "We need to find a way to prove it, because if we don't, you could spend up to five years in prison." I shook my head and closed the file. I wasn't going to prison for something I didn't do. As I stood up to leave, the contents from my purse fell to the floor. Tamela helped me to retrieve the items, laughing when she saw my cell phone and asked when I was going to upgrade. I laughed and told her that my daughter has been asking the same question every week.

Suddenly, Tamela's expression changed. She asked me if I had a reason not to trust her. Confused, I said no. She then showed me the phone and asked why I was recording our conversation. I sat on the floor and immediately started praying. I explained to her that my phone was old and any hard hits or drops on the floor would cause the phone to start recording. I took the phone out of her hand and reviewed all past recordings, and as fate would have it, we heard a recorded message with

Michelle's voice thanking me for selling her the office furniture and asking if I could hold the 75.00 check until Friday. I found the proof I needed.

The charges against me were dropped, Michelle was arrested for filing a false police report and terminated from the job. I was re-offered my position as well as an apology. I accepted the apology but declined the position. Instead, I decided to return to school to pursue a doctoral degree. Hopefully, Michelle learned a lesson from this experience, I sure did.

Love is Blind

Jade and Stan met in college. By the fourth year, they were deeply in love and planning to be married. Jade graduated within four years, but Stan stopped attending classes and eventually dropped out. He said he was fine with just getting a job, yet, Jade had some concerns because she did not want to be the kind of wife who was taking care of the bills and the man. After graduation, she was hired as the Business Operations Manager for Simpkins Public Accounting Firm, but the job was located in the next county, which caused her to arrive home late most evenings.

For six months, she had no idea that Stan had been fired from his job as a truck driver; he was involved in an on-the-job accident and had to take a drug test as a precaution. He tested positive for cocaine use and was terminated immediately. The very thing she feared was now a reality, she was taking care of the bills and the man.

Although she was disgusted by her home life, she did love Stan very much and was willing to remain loyal, devoted to making her marriage work. After about eight months, she noticed strange people at her home, staying no longer than five or six minutes. She asked Stan what was going on and he told her that he was taking care of business. These strange visits continued for the next few months and her suspicions continued to grow as well.

One day, she decided to leave work early. As she drove home, she was praying that nothing was happening inside of her house that would end her marriage. Hopefully Stan was out looking for a job. After arriving home and parking her car, she walked slowly to the front door of the house. She could hear people talking and laughing inside. She opened the door and was shocked! There were four women walking around completely nude and wearing a face-mask, Stan was there telling them what to do and another man was there as well looking at something cooking in four pots.

When Stan saw me standing there, he immediately took me by the arm and walked me into our bedroom. I yelled, "What the hell is going on?" He told me to calm down and to let him explain. He said because he wasn't able to find a job, he had to come up with another way to make money to pay the bills. He explained that he hired a few women to cook crack cocaine so that he and his partner, B, can sell it. He said he's been doing this for the past nine months. Nine months! I felt as if I was going to faint, I couldn't believe what I was hearing. This could not be my life, my husband, my home. This was a bad dream, it had to be.

Just when I didn't think it could get any worse, it did. Stan asked me if one of the women could move into our home temporarily to help watch the products. If this didn't take the cake! I began to walk away, not believing what I just heard. My husband just asked me if another woman could move into our home as a security guard for his in-house drug business. He stood in front of the door refusing to allow me to leave. He tried to kiss me, he unbuttoned my pants and proceeded to place his hand in my underwear while whispering that he was doing all of this for me, for us. He pleaded with me to let him be the man I deserved and allow him to prove to me that he can give me the life I've always wanted. I caved, we made love on the bedroom floor, and I told him that I did not want to see any evidence of this drug life and I had better not find out that he is having an affair with the woman he is moving into our home. He assured me they were only friends, and her boyfriend is his business partner, the other man who was standing in the kitchen. The move was going to be temporary, only until his partner is able to move here from Miami, FL.

Amazingly, the money began to roll in. Stan

purchased a new car and a safe to keep his money. Stella

(the new roommate) seemed to be happily in love with her

new boo-thang. She was even more excited after learning

that she was three months pregnant. Although her

boyfriend seemed supportive, I did wonder why he couldn't

move her out of my house. I also wondered why the three

of them took monthly trips out of town together without

me. Stan said it was business and he didn't want me

involved. He said that I was too good for that life, and he

would die if something happened to me. Stan said my job

was to look pretty, and spend his money. I was satisfied

with that.

The trio was scheduled to go out of town at the end

of the week and would be gone for three weeks. Odd,

they've never been away that long. Oh well, business is

business. Besides, Keisha is supposed to come over this

weekend to go shopping with me. Keisha has been my best

friend since college and she said she really wanted to talk with me about something. Probably some new guy she met.

Stan and his crew left for Miami on Thursday morning and I made plans to hang out with Keisha. She arrived on Saturday afternoon and I was ready to spend money. Keisha asked if we could just sit and talk for a few minutes before going to the mall. She held my hands and told me something I could never have imagined. She told me the man who is out of town with Stella and Stan wasn't the father of Stella's child. Keisha explained that Stan and Stella have been friends for more than nine years, they met at a strip club in Miami. Stella was also selling cocaine and that's how Stan started using cocaine.

Stunned, I said, "Wait, what do you mean using cocaine?" According to Keisha, Stan has been using for many years. Keisha said she found out about Stan and Stella three days ago and wanted to make sure the information was factual before she told me anything. She said she followed them, took pictures, and a video as well. The video showed Stan and Stella holding hands while shopping for the baby, he even spoon fed her ice cream while they ate lunch. In the video, the two of them were seen shopping for baby blankets at a store that embroidered personal messages on baby items.

Jade sat in the chair shocked. She couldn't believe it, her husband had moved his girlfriend into the bedroom down the hall, and at some point impregnated her in their home. Jade lowered her head into her hands and started to cry. She said to Keisha, "How could he do this to me, in our home? Another woman? How?"

Calmly, Keisha continued to explain, "After they left the embroidery shop, I went there pretending to shop for Stella's baby shower. The cashier told me that Stella was there earlier to order a baby blanket. I told the cashier that I did not want to order the same thing, so I asked if I could see the order form. The message on the order form read, 'Uncle Stan will always love you.' The cashier told me that Stella was there with her brother-n-law. Jade, the man you think is the father of Stella's child is actually her brother. His name is William Blakely, both he and Stella are from Miami. Stan is not having an affair with Stella, he's having an affair with William. They are in Miami this week to close on a house they are purchasing together."

Just as Keisha completed her sentence, there was a knock on the door. "Are you Jade Blackwell?" asked a casually dressed young man.

"Yes, I am," Jade, responded.

As she stood there, the man handed her a thick envelope and said, "You've been served," and quickly walked away.

Keisha stood beside her and asked, "What's up?"

Jade continued to stand in the doorway feeling numb. Keisha took the envelope from Jade's hand and read the contents, she then looked at Jade, but before Keisha could say anything, Jade said, "You don't have to tell me,

he's filed for a divorce."

Freedom and Friendship

Ronnie and Benji met eight months ago at the local gym. They seemed to have a lot in common and they both liked the same type of women; intelligent, independent, and thick! They went out a couple of times a month for drinks and conversation. The friendship was solid.

Benji was born and raised in Orlando, FL but I moved here two years ago after receiving the job transfer I applied for. The city is nice. The population is diverse, there are multiple theme parks, tourist attractions, great restaurants, and so much more. The best thing about living in Orlando is the weather; it's always warm and sunny, just the way I like it.

Ronnie arrived at Benji's apartment at 10:30 a.m. He was scheduled to catch a 2:00 p.m. flight to Boston, MA. As Benji walked toward Ronnie's car, he yelled, "Ronnie! What's up, man? Thanks for coming to pick me up, I can't afford to miss my flight. I really appreciate this.

I'll just put these two bags in the trunk of your car, but if you don't mind, before we go to the airport I need you to take me to my friend's place to drop them off. He left some clothes and books at my place last week and I promised to return everything to him before I leave for Boston."

"No problem, we have time. I need to put some gas in the car first. There's a station at the end of the next block," Ronnie said. As he drove away from Benji's place, he noticed a car speeding through a stop sign. The driver was a middle-aged white female. As they made eye contact, she slowed her car, called him a shiftless nigger, and erratically drove away. Ronnie, then said to Benji, "Bruh, how the hell can you stand living in this neighborhood with people like that? I mean, that woman didn't even know us, but we are shiftless niggers? Why? You need to move from this shit, man, quick."

Benji laughed out loud and said, "I feel you on that, but I'm telling you it's pretty peaceful over here. I don't hear gunshots every ten minutes, the cops aren't cruising the streets, and I don't worry about people breaking in and stealing my shit when I'm not home. I'm telling you, it's nothing but peace over here in these parts. As long as people mind their business, they don't have to like me, just let me live in peace. That's all I need. You feel me?"

"So, I guess being called a shiftless nigger for no reason is your definition of peace," said Ronnie.

Benji replied, "You right, you right. However, you have to admit this neighborhood is a lot safer than most places you've seen since you moved here. Remember when we were visiting Sherice, and someone broke into your car and stole your CD player and your brand new Jordans? That would never happen over here. Plus, smoking on these fat blunts help me deal with anything and anybody. You need to hit this a couple of time and relax your mind."

Looking confused, Ronnie said, "Bruh, first of all, you need to stop smoking so much and second, white people don't even wear Jordans!"

As they drove into the parking lot of the gas station, Benji agreed to pay for the gas. After Ronnie dove to an open pump, Benji left the car and walked into the gas station. As Ronnie was about to get out of the car, he noticed two police cars parking behind him. One of the officers walked to the driver side of Ronnie's car, the other officer remained at the rear. Ronnie asked if there was a problem and the officer said, "We received a complaint about a driver who attempted to run another car from the road a couple of blocks over. You know anything about that?"

Ronnie replied, "No, I don't." The officer then asked to see Ronnie's license, registration, and proof of insurance. As Ronnie reached into the glove compartment to retrieve the items, the officer asked him to move slowly.

He then asked if there were any weapons or illegal drugs in the car, and Ronnie said no. The officer took the paperwork and walked to his car.

After about fifteen minutes, he came back to Ronnie's car, he asked if Ronnie had been smoking Marijuana and again, Ronnie replied, no. The officer then explained that he could smell marijuana and the smell gave him probable cause to search the car. He asked Ronnie to step out of the car and hand him the keys. Ronnie complied and waited for the search to end. The officer opened the trunk and noticed two large bags, one of them was open, and some of the contents had fallen out. The officer called his partner and they both looked at Ronnie. They motioned for Ronnie to come to the back of the car, they asked if the bags and the contents were his and Ronnie yelled, "Hell no, that shit is not mine."

In the trunk of his car were two large duffel bags filled with OxyContin, and two types of date rape drugs,

Rohypnol and Gamma-hydroxybutyric acid (GHB).

Ronnie felt sick, he knew the drugs weren't his, these had

to be the bags Benji put in the trunk earlier.

Ronnie explained to the officers, "Look, my boy

just walked in the store to pay for my gas, he's right in

there and I'm sure he can explain this situation to you. This

is not my stuff. This is my car, but these drugs aren't mine.

You can give me a lie detector test, do whatever,

but I cannot go down for something I didn't do. I have

never been arrested, I am a college graduate, I have a job, I

just bought my first home, and I am not a drug dealer or

any other kind of criminal."

One of the officers agreed to walk into the store to

look for Benji. He talked with the store's owner but walked

out alone. The officer stated there was no one in the store,

but there was one black male in there earlier who asked to

use the bathroom shortly after the officers arrived. When

the officer went to check the bathroom, no one was there,

but there was an open window. Ronnie dropped to his knees. After a short time, the officer helped him to stand to his feet and then said that Ronnie was being placed under arrest. Ronnie kept shaking his head, now crying, insisted the drugs did not belong to him. As the officer placed the handcuffs around Ronnie's wrists, he read the Miranda Warning, "You have the right to remain silent. Anything you say can and will be used against you in a court of law. You have the right to an attorney. If you cannot afford an attorney, one will be provided for you. Do you understand the rights I have just read to you?"

Ronnie continued to sob as he was placed in the back of the police car. Soon a larger police vehicle arrived containing drug sniffing dogs. The dogs walked around Ronnie's car, stopped, jumped up and barked at the car's trunk. A photographer was there to take pictures, and as the officer drove away with Ronnie in the back seat, he could see the drugs as they were removed from the trunk of his car. He was devastated.

Although Ronnie was a first-time offender, he was still sentenced to 25 years in prison for the drugs found in his car. Ten months after Ronnie was sentenced, Benji was found dead in his apartment. He had been shot in the back of the head, execution style. A safe had been found in the closet of his bathroom, and it still contained more than 50,000.00 in cash. Nothing had been taken from the apartment; the shooter came there for one reason only, to get rid of Benji. But why?

Ten years after Ronnie's incarceration, one of the arresting officers went to the prison to visit him. Ronnie walked into the visitation room and was shocked to see the officer. As he slowly sat on the metal bench, he asked the reason for the officer's visit. The officer told him that he often thought about the day Ronnie was arrested. He explained that his gut told him that Ronnie was innocent, but with the amount of drugs in the car, he had to arrest him. He also believed the drugs belonged to Benji, especially due to his extensive drug related criminal record, but there was no proof the drugs in Ronnie's car belonged to Benji. On the witness stand Benji denied ownership of the drugs, and actually cried because he did not want to see his friend go to prison. Nevertheless, he still did not admit guilt.

Ronnie told the officer that life has been hell for him in prison. He had been raped four times, stabbed twice, and was informed last week that he was HIV positive. His family and friends no longer visit or write to him. Recently, one of the guards set him up to be beaten by three other inmates after Ronnie witnessed the guard give a cell phone to an inmate. Ronnie sat at the table and cried, feeling hopeless. The officer promised him that he would return the following week to visit him. He told Ronnie to stay strong and not to lose hope.

Two weeks later, the officer arrived at the prison with a box of files. He was excited to visit with Ronnie and couldn't wait to see him. When the door opened, the prison warden walked in without Ronnie. She explained, "I'm sorry to inform you of this, but Ronnie committed suicide last night. He was raped three nights prior while taking a shower. He sustained multiple injuries including internal bleeding as a result of the sexual assault." She then asked about the files in the box.

The officer sat silently while shaking his head and then told her, "I found proof that the prosecutor knew the drugs did not belong to Ronnie. Apparently, three months after Ronnie was sentenced, Benji walked into the prosecutor's office and confessed. He told her the drugs were his and he was supposed to deliver them to his boss the day Ronnie was arrested. When Benji went inside to pay for the gas, he saw the police searching the car and knew the drugs would be discovered. He went into the bathroom, called a friend to pick him up, and jumped out of the bathroom window.

After Ronnie was sentenced, Benji was overwhelmed with guilt and decided to tell the truth. The prosecutor, on the other hand decided not to disclose the information, but she did not throw Benji's written statement away, she simply placed it in a folder and filed it in an evidence box and marked it as a closed case. Evidently, someone from Benji's drug circle discovered that he confessed, and decided to have him killed. As it turns out, three months after Ronnie was sent here, the prosecutor had evidence to prove his innocence; yet, she said nothing about it and allowed an innocent man to sit in prison for 10 years. Now, you're telling me he's dead. What kind of justice can he receive at this point?"

A Bully's Remorse

Shauna hates school. Each morning, she begs her parents to keep her home and to enroll her in a homeschool program. Each morning, her parents object to the idea and encourages her to ignore the students who are bothering her. Since the third week of school, the same group of girls has bullied Shauna and no one seems to care. Her math teacher told her to walk away to avoid being suspended. The science teacher told Shauna that all kids are bullied, that it was a part of growing up. The physical education teacher told her to run in the other direction or learn to fight back. Today, however, will be very different for Shauna and her family.

As Shauna left her science class, she realized she left one of her books in the classroom. She immediately returned to the room to retrieve it. She thought it was weird that the lights were turned off and the teacher had left the room so soon after releasing the students, but she needed the book so she walked toward her desk. Just as she reached the third row where her desk was located, she heard someone laughing. She turned around and noticed Tessa, Sloan, and Meeka. Sloan walked up to Shauna and pushed her to the floor while the other girls laughed. Sloan then accused Shauna of spreading rumors about her and warned her to keep her name out of her mouth. As Shauna tried to get up from the floor, Tessa kicked her in the stomach and Meeka poured a warm liquid over Shauna's head. The girls laughed and threatened to do worse if Shauna told anyone what they did to her.

As she lay on the floor trying to breathe, she could smell the liquid and quickly realized it was urine. Her hair and face were saturated with urine! As soon as she was able to breathe, she stood up and punched Meeka in the face. At that moment all three girls began to hit and kick Shauna until she was unconscious. Sloan looked at Shauna's lifeless body and said, "I bet your smart ass won't be no doctor now!" The girls walked slowly away from the classroom trying not to be noticed; it worked, no one saw them as they carefully blended into the crowd of students in the gym.

Dr. Elaine Brown was walking to the hospital cafeteria when she was paged to the operating room. She quickly turned around and ran to the elevator. When she arrived at the desk, she was informed that a female juvenile was transported by ambulance and she had massive head and face trauma. As Dr. Brown prepared to enter the room to examine the patient, she began to tremble and scream. It was at that moment she realized the juvenile who was being prepared for surgery was her daughter, 16-year-old LaShauna Brown. Dr. Brown was forcefully removed from the operating room as she tried desperately to hug her daughter. Another emergency room doctor was running toward the room as Dr. Brown continued to cry and beg the nurses to let her see her baby.

Ten minutes later, two police detectives walked into the vacant hospital room to talk with Dr. Brown who was being comforted by the nurses. The first officer, Detective David Lucas kneeled beside her and gently explained what happened to her daughter. The second officer, Detective Shymir Habib stood quietly and observed all occupants as they remained in the room. Finally, Dr. Elaine Brown, as she continued to sob, asked if someone would contact her husband. With trembling hands, she wrote a number on a sheet of paper and handed it to Detective Habib, who quickly walked out of the room. After about 20 minutes, he returned and stated that Mr. Solomon Brown was driving to the hospital. Detective Lucas asked Elaine if Shauna had told her about any issues involving other students at the school, and Elaine nodded her head. Eventually she said, "My daughter has been complaining about a couple of girls, but I thought it was just regular high school stuff. I had no idea it was this bad or that the issues would result in my daughter being injured."

It was at that moment Detective Habib explained, "Ma'am, many times when children are telling their parents about being bullied at school, several parents think about their own past experiences and seem to think that today's bullying is the same, it's not. Some children go to school with feelings of anger, depression, envy, and many other emotions, and some of those children have no outlet.

I'm not making excuses for those who were involved in assaulting your daughter, but I am trying to explain how bullying today is extremely different from the level of bullying that we may have experienced. Nevertheless, I can assure you, we will continue to investigate this crime until your family receives justice."

Suddenly, a dark skinned man who stood about 6'7, with a broad chest, and muscular arms walked into the room. He immediately removed his pinstriped jacket and grabbed his wife to hold her tightly. It was at that moment, the detectives realized the man standing before them was Mr. Solomon Brown, Elaine's husband. He immediately asked, "Where is my baby girl? What's happened to her? I need to see Shauna, please."

Detective Lucas explained the circumstances of Shauna's assault and told both parents that she was in surgery to repair the head and face trauma she suffered during the attack. Three hours later, a doctor entered the room and explained that Shauna's surgery was successful. She continued to explain that Shauna would need 24-hour care from a nurse after she is released from the hospital. Her injuries were extremely severe and she would need to learn to walk and talk again. Elaine fainted.

Thirty Years Later

"Somebody, help me, please, help me! My baby been shot!" A lady ran into the emergency room and pointed to a car parked in front of the glass doors of the hospital. Immediately, five nurses ran toward the car.

Inside, was a young woman with bullet wounds to her upper torso. One of the nurses yelled, "Page Dr. Allen, now!"

After hearing her name over the hospital's intercom system, Dr. Allen ran toward the emergency room desk. As she arrived, she could see a badly injured woman being transported to the operating room. The injured woman was 28-year-old Shamika Brooks. Shamika was shot four times in the chest by her mother's boyfriend. Apparently, after years of being sexually molested by him, Shamika decided to fight back. She gained that courage after she walked into the bedroom and caught him standing naked attempting to force his penis into the mouth of her four-year-old son, Wendell. She pushed Wendell out of the room before the fight began.

Dr. Allen began to assess the damage caused by the bullet wounds and discovered that two of the bullets exited Shamika's back, the third and fourth bullets severed parts of her spinal cord. Shamika would be permanently paralyzed. As she prepared to break the news to Shamika's family, she heard loud screams coming from the direction of the waiting room. She walked quickly toward the sounds and saw several family members crying as four police officers tried to calm them.

The officers had just informed them that Shamika's son, Wendell was found unresponsive in the trunk of a car that crashed into a local lake. The driver (the boyfriend of Shamika's mother) was involved in a high-speed chase trying to avoid being arrested for attempted murder. Sadly, the family was also informed that Wendell had been shot in the abdomen before being placed in the trunk. The driver, however, died from a single gunshot wound to the head, subsequently causing the car to crash into the lake.

As the ambulance arrived with the small body of an African-American male child laying on the stretcher, Dr. Allen prepared for the worst. Suddenly, one of the emergency medical technicians yelled, "We have a pulse, he's breathing!" Dr. Allen leaped into action, the child was immediately taken to the operating room; the bullet was removed, there was no water in the boy's lungs, and there was no major internal organ damage. Dr. Allen looked toward the ceiling and thought to herself, *God is still in the business of performing miracles.*

Once again, she walked the long hall leading to the waiting room. Upon entering, she said, "I'm looking for the family of Shamika Brooks." To her surprise, everyone in the waiting room stood up.

The dominant woman in the room walked toward Dr. Allen and said, "I'm Ms. Brooks, Shamika's mother, but you can call me Sloan. Please, tell me you were able to save my baby, please! Doctor, is she gone live? What about my grandson?"

Dr. Allen proceeded to explain Shamika and Wendell's medical condition. When she was finished talking, Sloan gave Dr. Allen a tight hug and thanked her for saving the lives of her daughter and grandson. Sloan became confused by Dr. Allen's reaction to the hug. After gently pushing her away, Dr. Allen looked Sloan in her eyes and said, "God is responsible for saving the lives of your family, just as He was responsible for saving my life after you and your friends beat and kick me until I was unconscious. What? You didn't realize it was me?

Allen is my married name, Brown is my maiden name. I am Dr. LaShauna Brown-Allen, the same one that you said would never be a doctor, as I laid on a cold classroom floor dying. Well, as you can see, I was still able to live the life I planned for myself, and although I've forgiven you and your friends, I still hope you are getting everything in this life that you deserve." Dr. Allen walked away with a big smile on her face, and joy in her heart because as her mother always says, 'God is still in the business of performing miracles.'

Thirty Years Ago

Tessa Harris was arrested and charged as a juvenile for the assault of LaShauna Brown. After agreeing to testify against her co-defendants, Tessa only received a sentence of two years in a juvenile facility and an additional five years on probation.

Meeka White was arrested for the assault of LaShauna Brown and charged as an adult. She was sentenced to serve five years in an adult prison, where she was murdered by a gang member six months after her incarceration.

Sloan Brooks was also arrested for the assault of LaShauna Brown and charged as an adult. She was sentenced to serve ten years in an adult prison. During her incarceration, she was raped by a prison correctional officer, which resulted in a pregnancy. She later gave birth to a baby girl and named her Shamika Brooks.